# Be Positive!

**Cheri J. Meiners**

★

**illustrated by Elizabeth Allen**

free spirit
PUBLISHING®

**Library of Congress Cataloging-in-Publication Data**

Meiners, Cheri J., 1957–

    Be positive! / Cheri J. Meiners, M.Ed. ; Illustrated by Elizabeth Allen.

        pages cm. — (Being the best me)

    Audience: Ages 4–8.

    ISBN-13: 978-1-57542-441-5 (paperback)

    ISBN-10: 1-57542-441-X (paperback)

    ISBN-13: 978-1-57542-452-1 (hardcover)

    ISBN-10: 1-57542-452-5 (hardcover)

    ISBN-13: 978-1-57542-635-8 (ebk)

1. Optimism in children—Juvenile literature. 2. Attitude (Psychology)—Juvenile literature. 3. Positive psychology—Juvenile literature.  I. Allen, Elizabeth (Artist) illustrator. II. Title.

    BF698.35.O57M45 2013

    155.4'191—dc23

                         2013011668

Reading Level Grade 1; Interest Level Ages 4–8;
Fountas & Pinnell Guided Reading Level H

Cover and interior design by Tasha Kenyon
Edited by Marjorie Lisovskis

10 9 8 7 6 5 4 3 2 1
Printed in Hong Kong
P17200613

**Free Spirit Publishing Inc.**
Minneapolis, MN
(612) 338-2068
help4kids@freespirit.com
www.freespirit.com

To my adorable grandson Blake:
Your genuine smile is contagious.

I love waking up!
Each morning,
I can look forward
to a great new day.

I can choose to be positive.

I can decide to think happy thoughts
about people and things around me.

3

I'm grateful for all the good in my life.

When I smile or laugh,
I share my happiness with someone else!

I like to do new things all by myself,

and with other people.

I can do important things
with my head and hands,
and with my heart.

My body loves to move!

Being out in fresh air and sunshine helps me appreciate my world.

And when there is rain, wind, or snow,
I can find the positive in that, too!

Every season has something for me to enjoy.

I can look for all the good that people do.

I can thank those who care about me and help me.

Doing something nice for someone
can help me feel happy
faster than anything else.

17

Things won't always go the way I want,
but I can keep trying.

When things happen that I can't change,
I can talk to someone I trust.

I can choose to be patient
and accept the way things are.

Even when something seems bad,
I can learn from it or find some good in it.

I can find ways to make a difference.

When I try to help others feel happy,
I feel happy, too.

I can hope for great things in my future.

I can become the person I want to be.

What things will I do someday?

What will I be like?

29

I can choose to be positive and happy,
and expect the best.
I have the power to be
the very best me.

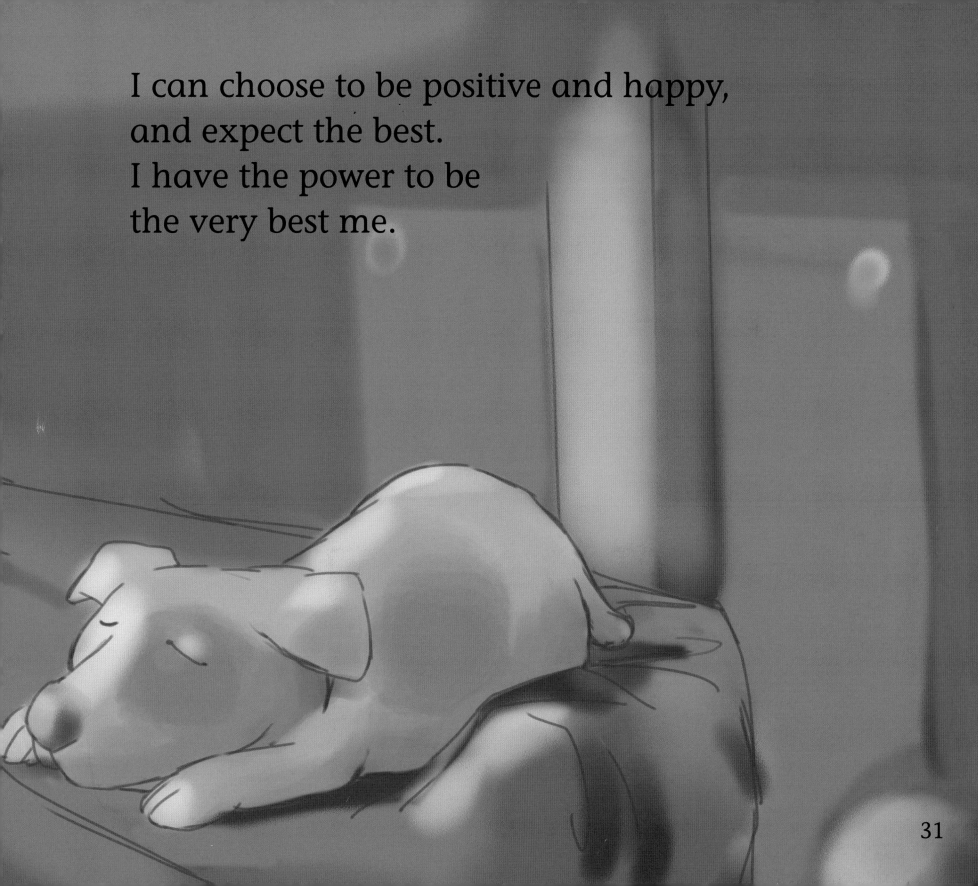

# Ways to Reinforce the Ideas in *Be Positive!*

*Be Positive!* teaches optimism, a perspective and outlook on life that leads to improved physical and mental health, better school performance, greater feelings of fulfillment, improved relationships, and a greater sense of control over one's life—all of which can lead to greater happiness. The purpose of the book is not to suggest that children ignore or deny sad or angry feelings, but to help them better understand their emotions and thought patterns and develop positive perspectives and skills for meeting their challenges. Children can learn optimism by becoming more familiar with their own patterns of thinking and adopting some of the principles discussed in this book and supported by the activities on pages 34–35. Here is a quick summary of optimism skills, most of which are mentioned in the children's text:

1. Be grateful for what you have.
2. Find what you like and are good at.
3. Make time to enjoy everyday pleasures.
4. Spend time outside and in nature.
5. Enjoy and talk with your family and friends.
6. Stay physically active.
7. Compliment others and be kind.
8. Be involved in things that are important.
9. Be patient with things you can't change.
10. Learn from your experiences.
11. Find the good and expect things to work out.
12. Do things that can make a difference.

## Words to know:

Here are terms you may want to discuss:

**accept:** to agree with or go along with something; to understand when something can't be changed

**appreciate:** to enjoy, to be grateful; to understand that something is important or good

**confident:** feeling strong, sure, and trusting

**expect:** to look forward to; to think that something can happen

**grateful:** appreciative or thankful; when you are grateful, you appreciate something and are glad for it

**patient:** able to stay calm and not complain when something is hard

**positive:** confident and hopeful; choosing to think happy thoughts

## As you read each spread, ask children:

- What is happening in this picture?
- What is the main idea?
- How would you feel if you were this person?

## Here are additional questions you might discuss:

**Pages 1–5**

- What did you look forward to when you woke up today?

- What things might this boy be grateful for? What are some things that are good in *your* life?

- How can smiling and laughing with someone be a way to share?

- If you are not thinking happy thoughts, how might you feel? Tell about a time when you chose to think happy thoughts. What happened? How did you feel?

**Pages 6–13**

- Tell about something new that you have learned. How did it feel when you could do it the first time?

- What is something you like to do by yourself? *(Answers might include: "Color a picture." "Choose what to wear." "Get dressed." "Pour my cereal.")*

- What is something you like to do with other people?

- What are some important things children can do? Why are these things important? How does it feel to do a good job at something that is important?

- How does your body like to move? How do you feel when you play and get exercise? How can exercise help you feel positive (about other things)?

- Some people think of rain, wind, or snow as "bad" weather. How does this boy see each kind of weather as something positive? What are things you like to do outside when it isn't sunny and warm?

- How can you turn a "bad" day into a good one—a positive one?

**Pages 14–17**

- What are some good things people do for you each day? Why do we thank people who do kind or helpful things for us?

- What is something nice that you can do for someone today? How do you think the person will feel? How can helping someone else help you feel more positive?

**Pages 18–25**

- When things don't go the way you want, why is it important to keep trying?

- If you had a problem, who could you talk to about it? How can talking about a problem help?

- When is a time you were patient? How did that feel?

- What are some things that won't last forever? How does knowing this help you be patient about things you don't like?

- Think of a little thing that might bother you. How might you look at it in a new way? *(Example: "I don't like my early bedtime. I can think about being able to get up early and rested so I can do what I want.")*

- Has something ever happened that seemed bad but later turned out to be good? Tell us about it. *(Example: "I didn't get to go to the store with my mom. My dad and I played together and ate ice cream.")*

**Pages 26–31**

- Think about a way that you can make a difference. What is a problem that you can do something about? *(Example: "I don't like arguing with my brother. I can stop teasing him.")*

- What is something you would like to do (or be) when you grow up?

- Why do you think things might work out if we expect the best to happen?

# Optimism Activities and Games

Read this book often with your child or group of children. Once children are familiar with the book, refer to it when teachable moments arise involving both positive behavior and problems relating to negative outlook and frustration. In addition, use the following activities to reinforce children's understanding of optimism and a positive outlook.

## Half Full or Half Empty?

Talk about the saying, "Some people see the glass as half full; others see it as half empty." Show children a "half full" glass of water, and discuss why some people see the same things but perceive them differently. Ask, "How would a person who is thinking positive thoughts describe it?" "Why do you think someone who thinks the glass is half full may feel happier?"

## Rose-Colored Glasses

Materials: Recycle an old pair of sunglasses, costume glasses, or 3-D movie glasses, taking out the lenses

Explain that "wearing rose-colored glasses" is a phrase that means someone sees everything as "rosy," or in a cheerful, positive way. Put on the glasses and tell positive things you notice about each child. Tell children, "Let's imagine that wearing these special glasses can help someone see positive things other people are doing." Let children take turns wearing the special glasses and giving positive comments. The glasses might also be worn by a child who is having a hard day.

## Positive Feedback

Optional materials (for Extension): Paper, envelope, and stamp for each child; pencils, crayons, markers

Directions: Have children sit in a circle. Discuss examples of positive comments. Then, one by one, have children give a positive comment to the person on their right. Each child can acknowledge the compliment with a smile and say "thank you." Be prepared to prompt appropriate comments, and accept all sincere attempts.

Extension: Ask children to think about someone who has done something kind for them. Have them write a letter or draw a picture that shares the child's positive thoughts and feelings. Assist children in giving or mailing the cards. Discuss how showing appreciation like this helps both people feel positive.

## Great Expectations Calendar

Materials: 8½" x 11" sheets of computer paper (13 sheets for each child); stapler or hole punch and yarn; pencils, crayons, markers; scissors, glue sticks, magazines (optional)

Each child will make a calendar with a page for each month and a cover page. The calendar may be made over several sessions. If desired, preprint the month names, or help children write them. Discuss common weather, holidays, and activities that occur each month. For each month of the next year, have children list, draw, or cut and paste magazine pictures of positive things to look forward to. Help children put the monthly pictures together into a calendar using the stapler or hole punch and yarn.

Variation: For younger children, make a single calendar page highlighting activities and events they can look forward to in the coming month, next week, or tomorrow.

## Positive Posting

Materials: Computer; blog site (free blogs can be set up at various sites such as blog.com, blogger.com, catchfree.com, tumblr.com, and wordpress.com; use privacy settings to allow access only to your group)

Directions: Have children practice cultivating positive thoughts by taking time to think about their day, what they liked, what went well, and why. Create a family or class blog and help each child record daily entries of things they felt good about or saw as positive. You may wish to upload pictures of some of the children's activities throughout the day.

Extension: Give children the opportunity to extend their practice of a positive outlook by helping them review other children's posts and add positive comments.

## Talk Show

**Materials:** Pen, 3" x 5" index cards, small plastic tub or paper bag, hand-held microphone (or you might improvise with a different prop to serve as a mic)

**Preparation:** On index cards, write simple situations, such as the scenarios listed below. Put the scenario cards in a plastic tub, paper bag, or other container. Set two chairs up front—one for the "talk show host" and one for a "special guest."

**Directions:** Tell children that they can have their own talk show. Invite a volunteer or appoint one child to be the "host" and another to be the "guest." The remaining children will be the audience.

Tell the host to draw a scenario card. Have or help the child read it aloud. Then have the host ask the guest, "How might this child feel?" "Why do you think so?" After the guest answers, the host asks the other children in the audience, "What (positive things) could this child say or do?" When a child raises a hand, the host brings the mic over for the child to use when answering. The host can "interview" as many children as desired before going to a new card or bringing up a new guest. If children need further prompting, you may wish to act as the first host, and prompt and help children rehearse answers before the "real show."

**Extension:** Write the children's responses on the back of the scenario cards. At a later time, have the children role-play the situations and their responses.

**Sample Scenarios:**

- Olivia's tower fell when she put on the last block.
- Noah didn't do well on his spelling test.
- Carlos was playing baseball, and he struck out.
- A child told Miriam that she couldn't play with the group.
- Suyin's teacher told her to stay in at recess to finish her work.
- Zachary tripped and hurt his knee.
- Ava's shoelaces were in a knot that she couldn't untie.
- Gabriel's dad said that he was too little to help mow the lawn.

## Positive Self-Talk

**Materials:** Sheet of cardstock, white paper, two markers (each a different color), scissors, magnets, whiteboard or chalkboard

**Preparation:** Draw and cut out a simple figure of a person from a page of cardstock. Decorate as desired. Using the white paper, draw and cut out several (16–20) thought bubbles. Take one-quarter or one-third of the thought bubbles and write one negative self-talk message on each, using one color marker.

**Directions:** When people lack confidence or feel depressed, they may be using negative "self-talk," or thinking negative thoughts such as the following: "I'm not old enough," "I'm not smart enough," "I'm too scared," or "It's too hard." Although much negative self-talk may seem like reality, children can be encouraged to build their optimism skills and confidence, find alternatives, and ask for help as needed.

Explain to children that a negative thought can often be replaced with a positive one. To play, put the cutout person on the board with magnets. Put up a negative self-talk message. Read or have a child read the message and ask children to tell a time when someone might feel this way. Then ask, "What is a positive way to see this?" Have children brainstorm positive thoughts that the child may use to counteract the negative one. As ideas are mentioned, write each on a thought bubble, using the second color marker, until you have two or three responses. Then let a child remove the negative thought that has been "pushed away" by the positive ones.

## Also in the Being the Best Me! Series

**Feel Confident!**
Empowers children to recognize their individual worth and develop confidence in themselves, their abilities, and the choices they make.

# Free Spirit's Learning to Get Along® Series by Cheri J. Meiners

Help children learn, understand, and practice basic social and emotional skills. Real-life situations, diversity, and concrete examples make these read-aloud books appropriate for childcare settings, schools, and the home. *Each book: 40 pp., color illust., S/C, 9" x 9", ages 4–8.*

**Accept and Value Each Person**
Introduces diversity and related concepts: respecting differences, being inclusive, and appreciating people just the way they are.

**Be Careful and Stay Safe**
Teaches children how to avoid potential dangers, ask for help, follow directions, use things carefully, and plan ahead.

**Be Honest and Tell the Truth**
Children learn that being honest in words and actions builds self-confidence and trust, and that telling the truth can take courage and tact.

**Be Polite and Kind**
Introduces children to good manners and gracious behavior including saying "Please," "Thank you," "Excuse me," and "I'm sorry."

**Cool Down and Work Through Anger**
Teaches skills for working through anger: self-calming, getting help, talking and listening, apologizing, and viewing others positively.

**Join In and Play**
Teaches the basics of cooperation, getting along, making friends, and being a friend.

**Know and Follow Rules**
Shows children that following rules can help us stay safe, learn, be fair, get along, and instill a positive sense of pride.

**Listen and Learn**
Introduces and explains what listening means, why it's important to listen, and how to listen well.

**Reach Out and Give**
Begins with the concept of gratitude; shows children contributing to their community in simple yet meaningful ways.

**Respect and Take Care of Things**
Children learn to put things where they belong and ask permission to use things. Teaches simple environmental awareness.

**Share and Take Turns**
Gives reasons to share; describes four ways to share; points out that children can also share their knowledge, creativity, and time.

**Talk and Work It Out**
Peaceful conflict resolution is simplified so children can learn to calm down, state the problem, listen, and think of and try solutions.

**Try and Stick with It**
Introduces children to flexibility, stick-to-it-iveness (perseverance), and the benefits of trying something new.

**Understand and Care**
Builds empathy in children; guides them to show they care by listening to others and respecting their feelings.

**When I Feel Afraid**
Helps children understand their fears; teaches simple coping skills; encourages children to talk with trusted adults about their fears.

**Learning to Get Along® Series Interactive Software**
Children follow along or read on their own, using a special highlight feature to click or hear word definitions. User's Guide included. *For Mac and Windows.*

**www.freespirit.com • 800.735.7323**
Volume discounts: edsales@freespirit.com • Speakers bureau: speakers@freespirit.com